BOOK REVIEWS

Here's what people are saying:

The brief text flows along smoothly for reading aloud or for independent reading. Zaunder's watercolors on white backgrounds have the cartoon and lightly humorous quality of Quentin Blake's drawings.

from SCHOOL LIBRARY JOURNAL

Children will like the parrot's silly rhymes and the cartoon illustrations.

from PORT HURON, MI TIMES HERALD

Weekly Reader Children's Book Club presents

Max, the Bad-Talking Parrot

Patricia Brennan Demuth

Illustrated by Bo Zaunders

Dodd, Mead & Company • New York

This book is a presentation of Weekly Reader Books.
Weekly Reader Books offers book clubs for children
from preschool through high school.
For further information write to:
Weekly Reader Books,
4343 Equity Drive, Columbus, Ohio 43228.

Published by arrangement with Dodd, Mead & Company.

Library of Congress Cataloging-in-Publication Data
Demuth, Patricia.   Max, the bad-talking parrot.
Summary: A misunderstanding causes a rift in the friendship between Mrs. Goosebump and Max the parrot, until a burglary brings an unexpected solution.   [1. Parrots—Fiction.   2. Burglary—Fiction] I. Zaunders, Bo, ill.   II. Title.   PZ7.D4122Max 1986   [E]   85-20572
ISBN 0-396-08767-1

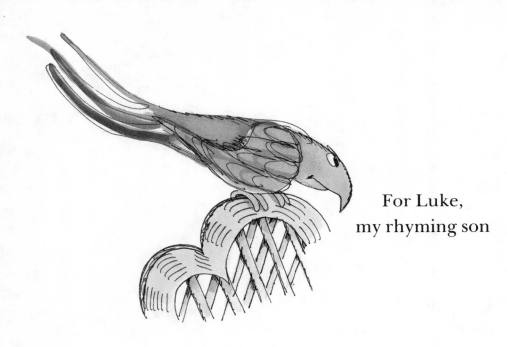

For Luke,
my rhyming son

Max was Tillie's parrot. He lived with Tillie on the bottom floor of a cozy two-story house. Their best friend, Mrs. Goosebump, lived on the floor above them.

Mrs. Goosebump worked nights at a tollbooth. All
night long, she sat alone in the small booth with no one
to talk to except the drivers who stopped to pay their
tolls. So, when work was done, Mrs. Goosebump liked
nothing better than to visit with Max and Tillie.

Each morning, when Max heard the doorbell ring, he would say:

*"Nine o'clock on the nose.
Mrs. Goosebump, I suppose."*

"I suppose," Tillie would answer, and sure enough, it was always Mrs. Goosebump.

"Hel-LO, dearies," Mrs. Goosebump
would call as she waltzed in. Tillie
would kiss her on the cheek, and Max
would fly to her and say:

*"Won't you let me take your hat?
Stay awhile and have a chat."*

Max would hang Mrs. Goosebump's hat on a peg. Then he would say:

> *"Do sit in the wicker rocker*
> *By the big old ticker-tocker."*

There was something special about Max, which you may have already noticed. Max talked in rhymes.

When Mrs. Goosebump was comfortable, Tillie would make apple-cinnamon tea, Mrs. Goosebump's favorite. Then Mrs. Goosebump would take a white bakery box out of her shopping bag. Max's eyes would grow big as he waited to see what was inside. Mrs. Goosebump always brought something with nuts, because Max loved nuts.

Max perched on her shoulder then and Mrs. Goosebump fed him. Max would make up a little rhyme, like this:

> *"I like nuts because they crunch.*
> *Crunch a bunch, you have a lunch."*

When the nuts were all gone, Max would snuggle
down on Mrs. Goosebump's shoulder for a nap. Tillie
and Mrs. Goosebump would finish tea and talk about
tenpin bowling, swimming at the Y, or the news in the
morning paper.

And that is how the three friends shared each
morning—until the big problem with Max began.

One morning, as Max awoke from his nap, he heard
Mrs. Goosebump say something terrible about him. He
heard Mrs. Goosebump say, "Max is an ugly bird."

Instantly Max flew to a far corner of the room. Mrs. Goosebump was startled. "Why, Max," she said, "did you have a bad dream?"

Max did not answer her. He headed straight for his cage and stayed there and didn't say anything, even when Mrs. Goosebump said softly, "Good-bye, Max. I hope nothing is wrong."

All day long, Max paced up and down in his cage. *Ugly!* The more he thought about it, the worse he felt. The worse he felt, the grumpier he got. He wouldn't make up rhymes for Tillie during tidy-up time. He only ate half his seeds for supper. Tillie hoped Max would be his old self in the morning.

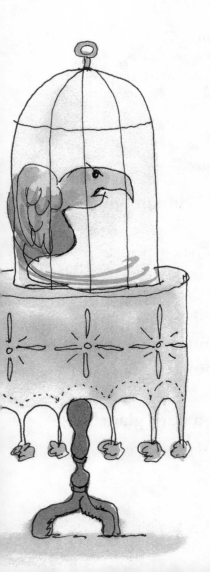

But the next morning, when Max heard the doorbell ring, he said:

> *"It's nine o'clock, I suppose.*
> *Mrs. Goosebump, go blow your nose."*

Tillie was astonished. "Max!" she cried. "What's gotten into you?" She opened the door and Mrs. Goosebump waltzed in, singing out her usual, "Hel-LO, dearies."

But Max answered:

> *"I say, I chirp,*
> *Did someone burp?"*

"Mind your manners, Max," Tillie scolded.

Mrs. Goosebump walked up to Max. "Whatever is the matter?" she asked.

Max turned away. He did not take her hat or invite her to sit in the wicker rocker. And during tea, he did not come out of his cage to eat nuts or make up rhymes.

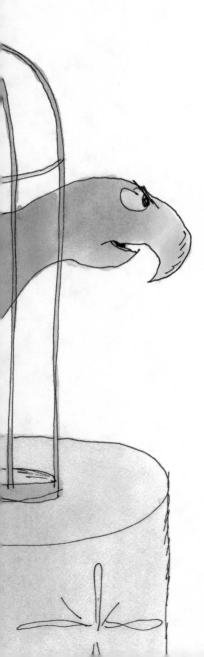

The next day was no better. When Mrs. Goosebump brought out the bakery box, Max said:

"Cupcake, bagel, cinnamon roll.
Your brain's as full as a donut hole!"

And the day after that, when Mrs. Goosebump waltzed in, Max said:

"Keep your hat—it's a disgrace.
It might look better over your face."

And when Tillie brought out the apple-cinnamon tea, Max said:

"Would you like something to stink—
I mean, to drink?"

Mrs. Goosebump had heard enough. She glared at Max. "I don't know what's wrong with you, Max," she said, "but I'm not putting up with any more of your bad talk. Tillie, let's have our tea upstairs."

"I guess we'd better," said Tillie. With a dark glance at Max, she picked up the tray and the newspaper, and followed Mrs. Goosebump out the door.

Max stomped back and forth in his cage.

"Go up there.
See if I care,"

he said to himself. But Max did care. He felt
as empty as the empty apartment.

Max did not see how things could get worse. But that night, they did.

While Tillie was bowling, a masked man crept into the apartment. A burglar! The man stuffed some of Tillie's things into a sack and went out. He came back with the sack empty. Once. Twice. On the third trip he looked at Max. "I must be nuts," he muttered, but he grabbed Max's cage too. He jammed it into the front seat of his van and sped away.

In minutes Tillie's apartment was far behind. The thief headed for the dark highway outside of town.

Poor Max. He crouched low in his cage, as far from the burglar as he could get. The dark shadows of Tillie's things stuck out all around him. Max closed his eyes and wished that everything was back where it belonged— including himself.

Then he felt the van begin to slow down. And then it stopped. Max opened his eyes.

The burglar was rolling down the window.
He reached into his pocket and handed out
some money.

Max heard a voice sing out, "Fifty cents
will be your change."

That voice! Max would know that voice
anywhere. It was Mrs. Goosebump! They
must be at her tollbooth. Max knew he had
to act fast.

As loudly as he could, Max called out:

"Howdy-doody!
You're a fruity!"

Mrs. Goosebump thought it was the
burglar talking to her.

"Did you call me a fruity?" she demanded.

"Uh, no. NO!" said the burglar. "I—I said you're a *cutie*!"

The burglar shook his hand for the change. He wanted to get going. Quickly Max shouted:

"Flying feathers in a hurricane!
What flew in? A real flea-brain."

Again Mrs. Goosebump thought it was the burglar talking to her. "Flea-brain! Is that what you called me?"

"No, NO!" the burglar sputtered. "I said, uh, uh—it looks like *rain*!"

Then Max shouted:

"Golly Nelly!
Something's smelly!"

"Oh!" roared Mrs. Goosebump.

"*Belly*!" yelled the burglar. "Mine's, er, empty. I'm hungry! So if you'll just give me my *change*…"

At that moment, Max got really smart. He yelled:

> *"Do sit in the wicker rocker*
> *By the big old ticker-tocker."*

"What?" cried Mrs. Goosebump. "That's Max's rhyme!"

The burglar still had his hand out. But instead of putting change in it, Mrs. Goosebump grabbed it—tightly. She leaned far out the tollbooth window.

"Just a minute here," she said. "That chair you've got in your van. That chair looks like Tillie's rocker. And that grandfather's clock. Why, that's Tillie's! And that voice I heard rhyming—that voice was Max! So you must be a burglar! I'm calling the police."

As Mrs. Goosebump reached for the
phone, the burglar stepped on the gas. The
motor roared. Tires screeched. The van
smashed through the toll gate. Sirens blared.
Lights flashed.

Max thought the burglar might get away,
but up ahead a line of police cars appeared.
The van had to halt.

As the burglar was being handcuffed, another police car raced up. Out jumped Mrs. Goosebump.

"Here's our hero," she said, lifting Max's cage from the burglar's van. "This is Max. His quick thinking caught the burglar!" She smiled at Max.

Max fluffed out his feathers with pride. He nodded at Mrs. Goosebump and told the policeman:

"No detective can top her.
She's a smart burglar stopper."

The policeman laughed. "I'd say you partners make a fine team."

Max and Mrs. Goosebump rode home in the back seat of a police car. Max snuggled down on Mrs. Goosebump's shoulder. He felt safe and warm. But after a few minutes, he began to think about what had been bothering him all week. He edged away from Mrs. Goosebump's cheek and said:

"Do you still think I'm an ugly bird?
You thought I was sleeping, but I overheard."

Mrs. Goosebump looked shocked. "You overheard me say you were ugly? But I never said such a thing!" For a long while, Mrs. Goosebump looked puzzled. Then she remembered something. "Max," she said, "that day you flew away from me, you thought I said you were ugly. Is that why you've been acting so bad?"

Max nodded.

"Max, you should have talked to me," Mrs. Goosebump said gently. "Then I could have told you that you had misunderstood. I did not say you were *ugly*. I said you were *snugly*."

Max's dark eyes blinked.

"*Snugly*," Mrs. Goosebump repeated.

Max let out a low whistle. He rolled his eyes. He shifted back and forth on her shoulder, shaking his head. After a moment, he said:

"Ketchup on burgers, mustard on weiners.
I'd better take my ears to the cleaners!"

Then he curled into the curve of Mrs. Goosebump's neck and winked at her. Mrs. Goosebump winked back.